MARVEL

CIVIL WAR
CAPTAIN AMERICA

CAPTAIN AMERICA
VERSUS
IRON MAN

Adapted by Chris Strathearn and R. R. Busse

Screenplay by Christopher Markus & Stephen McFeely

Produced by Kevin Feige

Directed by Anthony and Joe Russo

Illustrated by Ron Lim, Andy Smith, and Andy Troy

(L)(B)

LITTLE, BROWN AND COMPANY
New York Boston

marvelkids.com

© 2016 MARVEL

Little, Brown and Company

Hachette Book Group
1290 Avenue of the Americas, New York, NY 10104
Visit us at lb-kids.com

Little, Brown and Company is a division of Hachette Book Group, Inc.
The Little, Brown name and logo are trademarks of Hachette Book Group, Inc.

The publisher is not responsible for websites (or their content)
that are not owned by the publisher.

First Edition: April 2016

Library of Congress Control Number: 2016932126

ISBN 978-0-316-27140-0

10 9 8 7 6 5 4 3 2 1

CW

Printed in United States of America

JOIN UP WITH THE LIVING LEGEND

CAPTAIN AMERICA

Steve Rogers is the world's first Super-Soldier. He fought in World War II, but was frozen for years. Now he is an Avenger, fighting to save the world and help people as Captain America!

SIDE WITH THE INVINCIBLE

IRON MAN

Tony Stark is a billionaire and a genius. He invented his own suit of armor that can fly and blast villains. His armor is very strong, and can protect Tony from all kinds of attacks.

He is one of the leaders of the Avengers!

Natasha Romanoff is a super spy. She used to work with Captain America at S.H.I.E.L.D. as Black Widow. She's very smart.

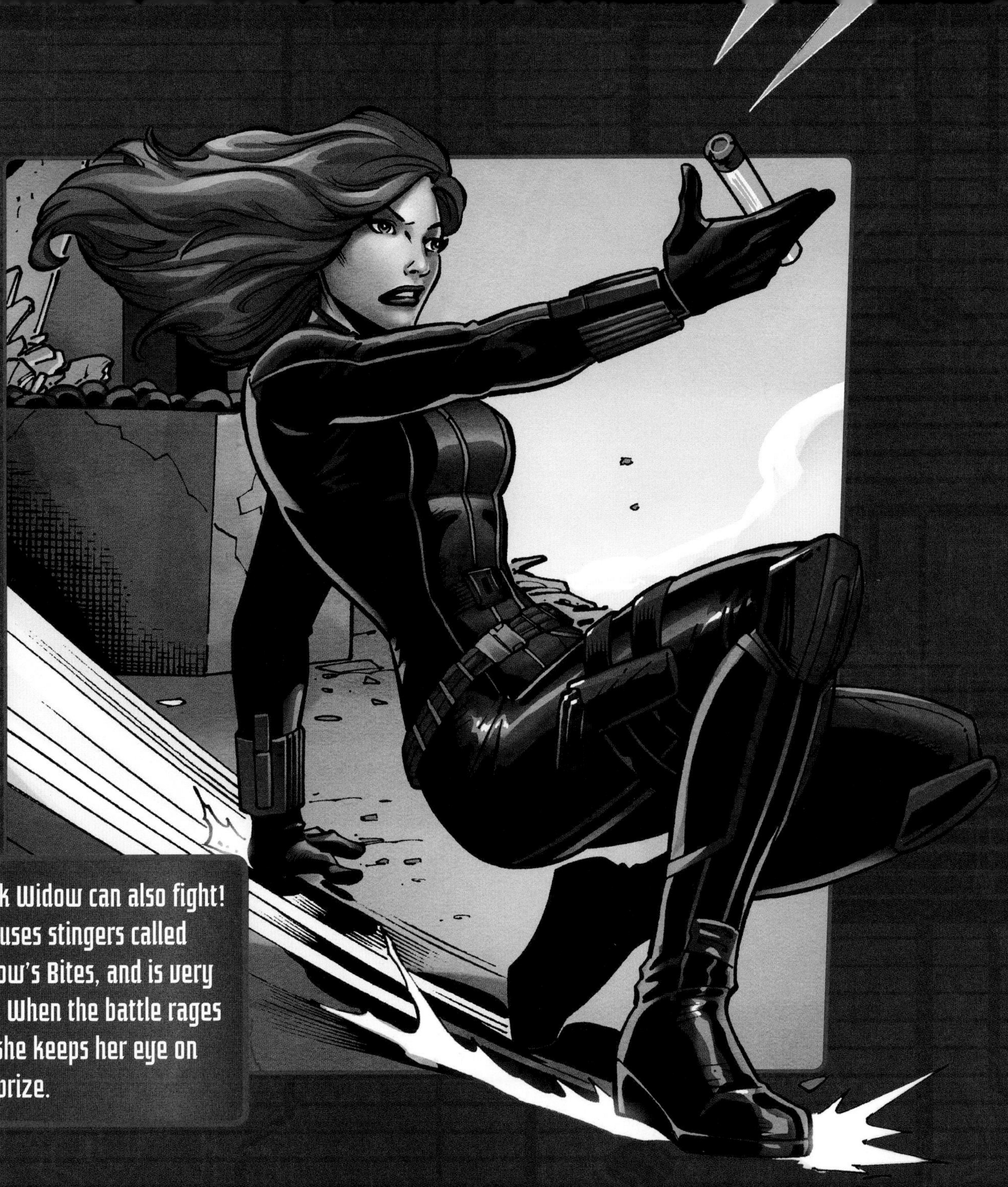

Black Widow can also fight! She uses stingers called Widow's Bites, and is very fast. When the battle rages on, she keeps her eye on the prize.

James "Rhodey" Rhodes is Tony Stark's best friend. He has a suit of armor a lot like Iron Man's. He can shoot missiles and fly, just like the original armored Avenger!

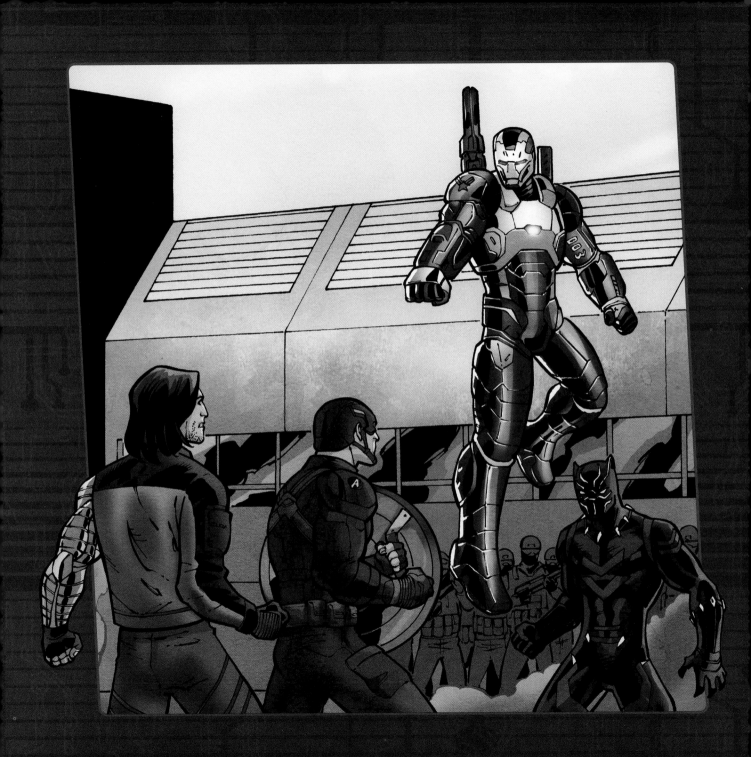

The Vision is part robot. He was created by Ultron, but now he is a good guy!

He can fly, phase through solid objects, and shoots a laser from the stone on his forehead.

BLACK PANTHER

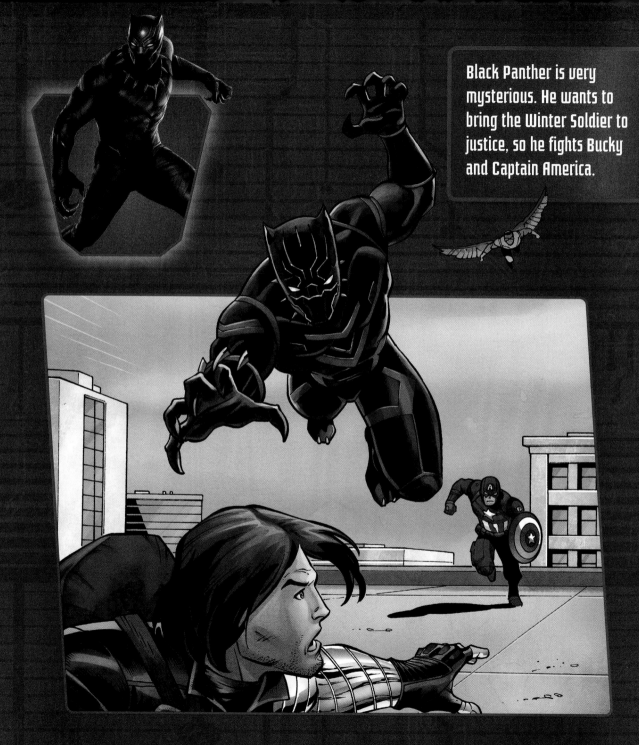

Black Panther is very mysterious. He wants to bring the Winter Soldier to justice, so he fights Bucky and Captain America.

He has very sharp claws that can actually scratch Captain America's shield!

FLIP THE BOOK
TO LEARN ABOUT

TEAM CAP

TEAM STARK

FLIP THE BOOK TO LEARN ABOUT

He has a metal arm that is very strong and fast. He is almost as good at fighting as Captain America!

WINTER SOLDIER

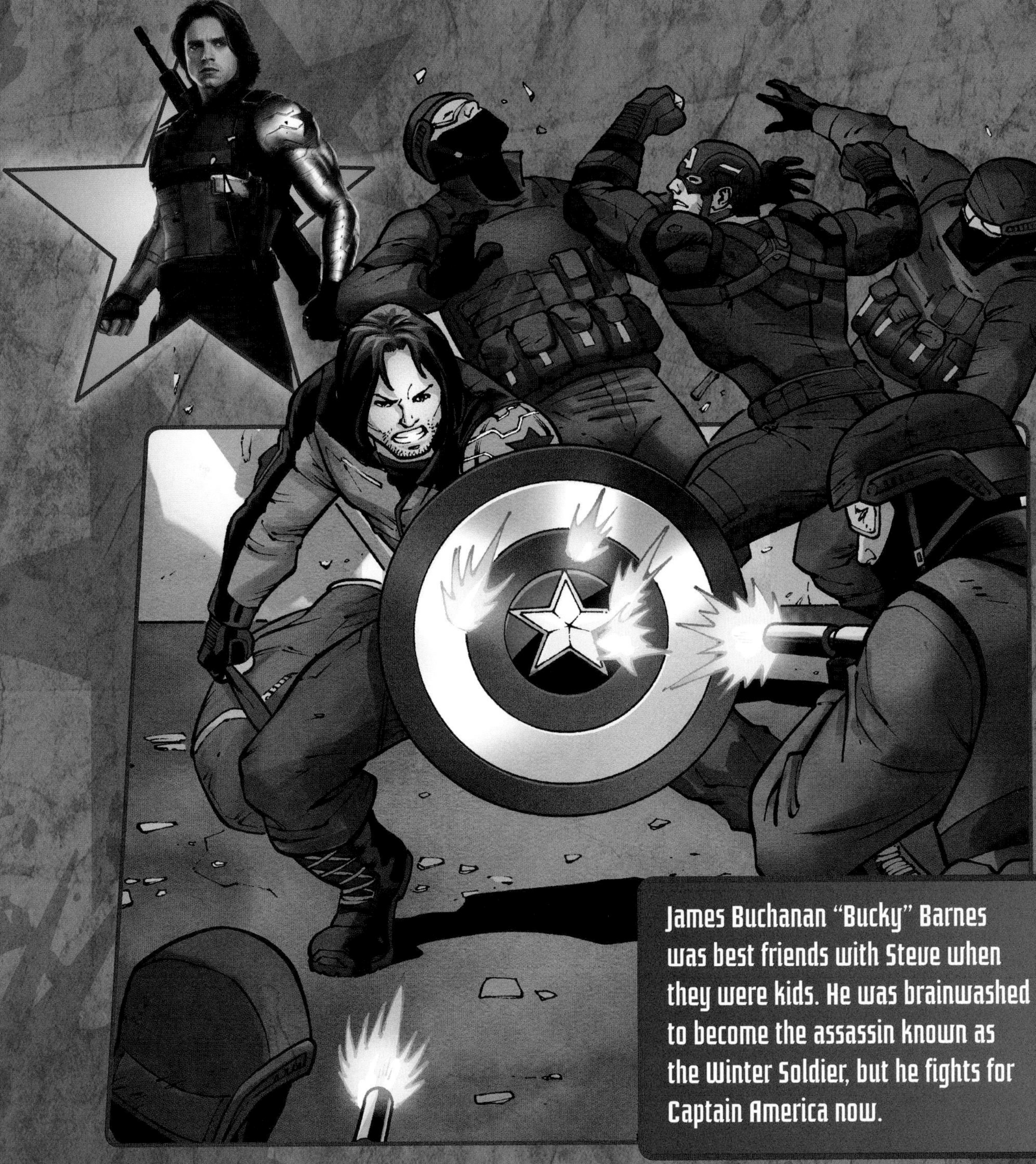

James Buchanan "Bucky" Barnes was best friends with Steve when they were kids. He was brainwashed to become the assassin known as the Winter Soldier, but he fights for Captain America now.

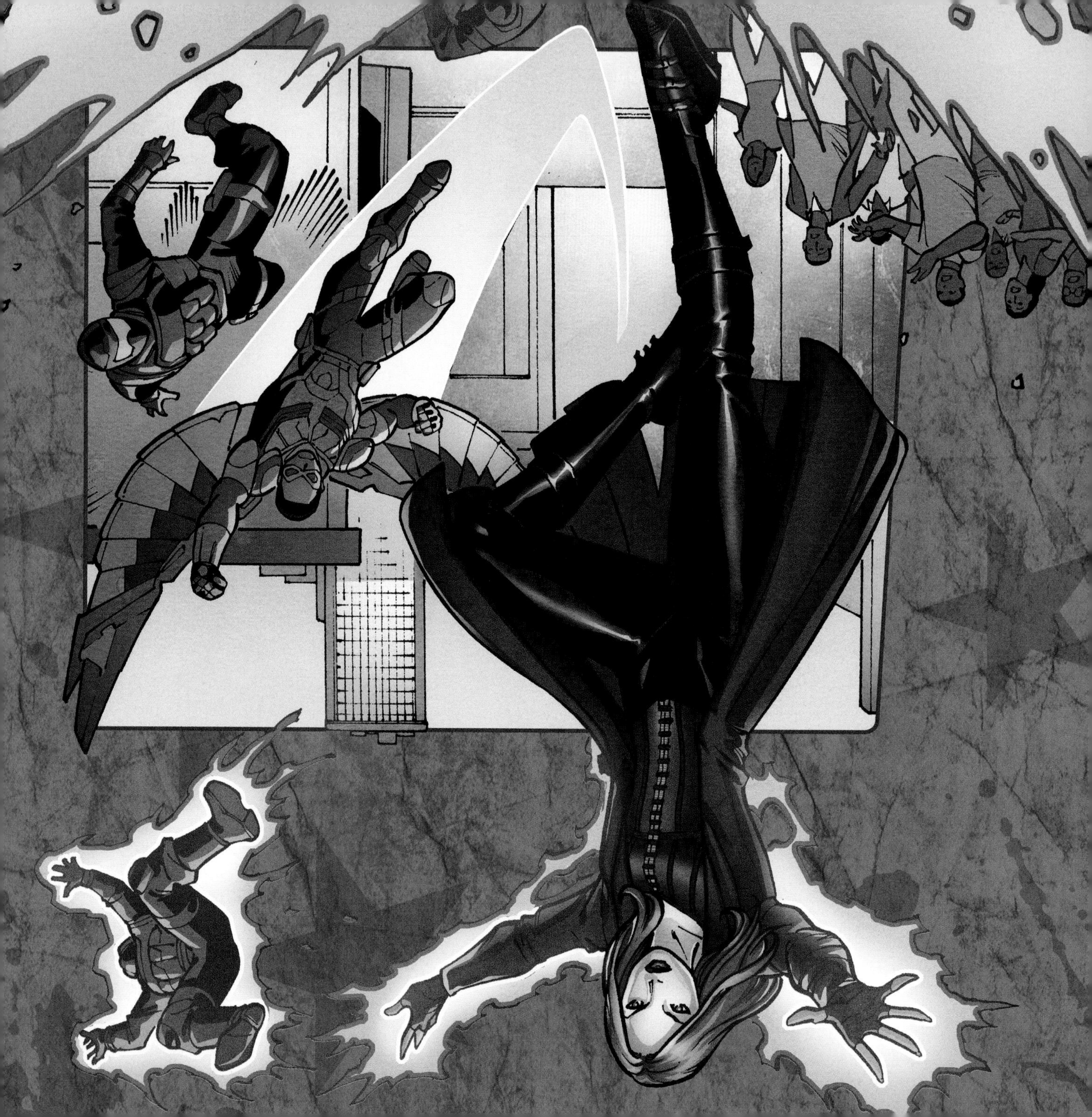

Wanda Maximoff used to work for the evil Ultron, but now she fights with Captain America to help people. She moves things with her mind, and goes by Scarlet Witch!

SCARLET WITCH

Falcon has a drone called Redwing that helps him. He watches his teammates' backs from the sky.

FALCON AND REDWING

Sam Wilson has metal wings that let him fly as Captain America's partner. He goes by Falcon, and is very brave.

He fights bad guys with a very strong shield, super strength, and advanced combat skills.